THE JUNGLE BOOK

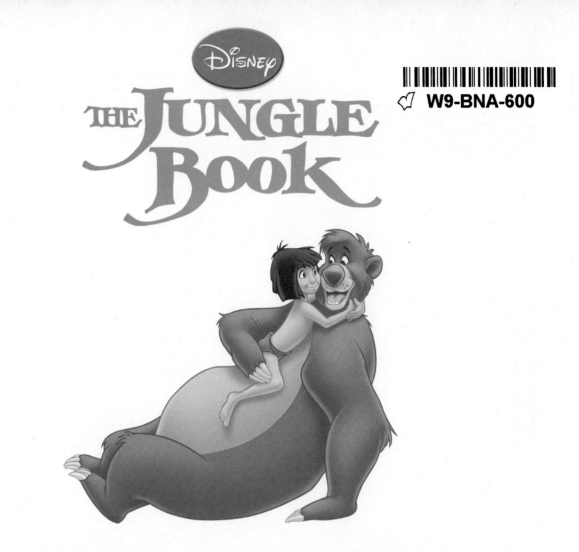

*This is the story of a little boy named Mowgli,
a big bear named Baloo, and a jungle journey—toward home.*

Jungle Book characters based on the Mowgli Stories in
The Jungle Book and *The Second Jungle Book* by Rudyard Kipling.

Deep in the jungle, Bagheera the panther was out hunting. He discovered a baby tucked inside a shipwrecked boat.

"Why, it's a Man-cub!" he thought. "This little chap needs food and a mother's care. Perhaps Mother Wolf will look after him."

Mother Wolf agreed to help. They named the Man-cub Mowgli, and he grew up safe and happy in the jungle.

Mowgli loved being a wolf pup. But everything changed when Mowgli was ten years old. Shere Khan, the man-eating tiger, heard about the Man-cub and came searching for him.

The wolves held an urgent meeting to discuss Mowgli's future. They agreed that Bagheera should take the boy to the Man-village where he would be safe.

The next morning, Bagheera and Mowgli set off on their long journey. Mowgli was angry and upset. He didn't understand why he had to leave the jungle—it was his home!

When darkness fell, Bagheera and Mowgli settled down to sleep in a tree. Nearby, Kaa, the snake, was hiding in some leaves. Kaa slithered toward the Man-cub.

Kaa's shining yellow eyes seemed to have a magic power on Mowgli. The boy sank into a deep trance. Kaa slowly wound himself around Mowgli, ready to swallow him up!

Suddenly, Bagheera woke up and sprang at Kaa. He gave the snake a terrible blow and sent him slithering away into the jungle.

At dawn, Mowgli ran off. Bagheera caught up with him and wanted to continue toward the Man-village. But Mowgli wouldn't go. He grabbed hold of a tree trunk and held on tightly. This made Bagheera very cross—and he ran off, leaving the Man-cub all alone.

But not for long! Mowgli met a friendly bear named Baloo.
"Well, now, what have we here?" Baloo asked.

Mowgli introduced himself. He told Baloo how he wanted to stay in the jungle.

"Well, Little Britches," said Baloo, "I'm going to show you!"

Baloo enjoyed teaching his new friend about the "bear necessities" of life. Soon Mowgli could fight like a bear, growl like a bear, and even scratch like a bear!

Later that afternoon, Mowgli and Baloo waded into the river to keep cool. As they floated along, Mowgli sat on Baloo's tummy, and the big bear fell asleep.

Monkeys were watching from the trees. They swung down and grabbed the Man-cub!

"Hey! Let go of me!" Mowgli shouted.

Baloo woke with a jump, but it was too late! The monkeys were already carrying Mowgli off to the ruined temple where they lived.

At the ruined temple, Louie, King of the Apes, offered to help Mowgli stay in the jungle. In return, he wanted the secret of Man's red fire.

Meanwhile, Bagheera had heard Mowgli's cries. He found Baloo, who explained what had happened. The two planned to rescue Mowgli.

King Louie declared they should have a great feast and dance in honor of Mowgli. Mowgli's feet began to tap to the music, and he joined in the fun . . . just as Baloo and Bagheera had reached the temple.

Who is this lady ape? Baloo! King Louie rushed over to ask the "lady ape" to dance. But as Baloo danced, his disguise began to fall off!

The monkeys realized they had been tricked—and a ruckus began! Bagheera rushed over to help and Baloo knocked down part of the temple. They grabbed Mowgli and ran to safety in the jungle.

"The Man-cub *must* go back to the Man-village," Bagheera insisted. "The jungle is not the place for him."

But the next morning, Mowgli ran off again!

Bagheera insisted that they would have to find Mowgli before Shere Khan did—not knowing that Shere Khan was close by . . . listening.

Shere Khan caught Mowgli's scent. He found him and leaped at him—and then jolted to a stop! Baloo had caught him by the tail!

Shere Khan roared with rage and flipped Baloo over his head. The bear hit the ground with a great thud.

Suddenly, lightning struck a nearby tree and it burst into flames. Shere Khan was terrified of fire!

Mowgli picked up a burning branch and tied it to the tiger's tail. Shere Khan screamed and fled into the jungle—never to be seen again.

Mowgli ran over to Baloo, who was lying very still.
"Baloo, get up!" Mowgli cried. "Oh, no! Baloo!"
Was Baloo dead?
No! Baloo sat up and rubbed his eyes. Mowgli
laughed and threw his arms round the big bear's neck.

A short time later, the three friends saw the Man-village on the other side of the river… and they heard someone singing. There at the river's edge was a young girl fetching water. This made Mowgli curious.

"I've never seen one before!" he said.

The girl turned and smiled. Mowgli shyly smiled back.

Baloo and Bagheera watched as Mowgli picked up the girl's water jug and followed her. Just before Mowgli walked through the entrance to the village, he turned to smile at his old friends.

"Mowgli is where he belongs," sighed Bagheera.
"Come on," said Baloo. "Let's get back to where *we* belong."

And as the sun set, the two friends headed back toward the jungle, singing and dancing happily.